SBE
FU

SORRY, MISS!

Jo Furtado · Frédéric Joos

Red Fox

SAT 27 JAN

Sorry, Miss Folio . . .

I took your book to my grandad's house . . .

and he read it to me lots of times and I thought it was really good and so did he . . .

and I left it there for him to read it to me again . . .

Only we haven't been back to Grandad's yet because he's got these horrible spots . . .

Sorry, Miss Folio . . .

We went to visit my grandad in hospital to see how his spots were and get your book back ...

but he'd lent it to another old man with his leg in plaster ...

and he'd lent it to the night nurse only she wasn't there ...

and my grandad says he doesn't like her because she keeps giving him tablets ...

SAT 24 MAR

Sorry, Miss Folio . . .

We went to the circus last Saturday and I took your book to read while I was waiting . . .

but I waved it at my friend and this huge elephant snatched it off me . . .

but my dad got it back only he'd sat on it by then . . .

and my mum is still trying to flatten it out for you . . .

Sorry, Miss Folio . . .

I was reading your book to the gnome in our garden because it's a good story . . .

and my mum called me in for tea and the gnome said he wanted to finish the book so I left it for him . . .

Only it rained and the book got a bit wet . . .

and my mum's still drying it out for you . . .

Sorry, Miss Folio . . .

Mum and Dad took me to the zoo and I took your book to read in the car . . .

and the first animal we saw was an ostrich . . .

and I don't like ostriches because he swallowed your book . . .

but the keeper said he'd spit it out soon only he hadn't by the time we came home . . .

Sorry, Miss Folio . . .

I put your book out ready to bring to the library but a burglar broke in last night . . .

and stole our video and my mum's purse and your book . . .

but we found your book on the path this morning . . .

only the policeman took it away to see if it had the burglar's fingerprints on it . . .

Sorry, Miss Folio . . .

My brother threw your book into
this enormous patch of nettles near
our house . . .

just because I threw his robot into
next-door's garden . . .

and next-door's dog got it . . .
and my dad says it serves me right

and no way is he risking life and
limb in those nettles even if it is the
best book in the whole world!

Sorry, Miss Folio . . .

I took your book to the beach when we went on holiday and my dad was rowing us across the bay...

when this octopus grabbed your book...

but my dad grabbed it back...

only somehow it got into my friend Catherine's luggage and she lives in Aberdeen...

SAT 29 SEP

Sorry, Miss Folio...

You know they're digging up the road outside the library ...

Well, I was looking into the hole in the ground when I dropped your book ...

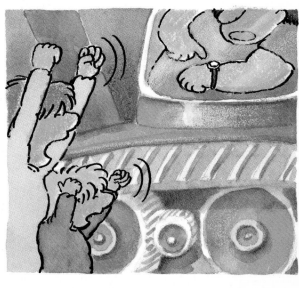

just as this big digger filled in the hole with earth ...

but the foreman promised my mum he'd dig it out for me only he can't till Monday ...

SAT 27 OCT

Sorry, Miss Folio . . .

We came down to the library on the bus today and I had your book . . .

but I got up to ring the bell and I left your book on the seat . . .

and this old lady shouted after me . . .

only I thought she was telling me off so I got off quick and the bus has gone to Manchester . . .

SAT 24 NOV

Sorry, Miss Folio...

My big brother tied your book to a rocket and sent it up in the sky . . .

and it came down in the old canal . . .

and my dad found it floating the next morning and he waded in and got very smelly . . .

only so is the book very smelly and my mum is getting rid of the pong for you . . .

Sorry, Miss Folio...

My mum says she was icing the Christmas cake last night...

when this strange man in red with a white beard...

came in and stole your book and flew away with it...

only that's a silly story isn't it—not as good as the one in your book...

For
Kalli who borrowed
Medi and Janet who loaned
and Arthur who read. (J.F.)

To Gahi, Emmanuelle and Kochi (F.J.)

A Red Fox Book

Published by Random House Children's Books
20 Vauxhall Bridge Road, London SW1V 2SA

A division of Random House UK Ltd

London Melbourne Sydney Auckland
Johannesburg and agencies throughout the world

First published by Andersen Press in 1987 under the title *Sorry, Miss Folio!*

Beaver edition 1989
Red Fox edition 1993

Text © 1987 by Jo Furtado
Illustrations © 1987 by Frédéric Joos

Printed in Italy by Grafiche AZ, Verona

ISBN 0 09 957180 3